THE HUNT FOR THE SAPHAEA

Esa & Sol's Adventures

Written by Asma Maryam Ali

Edited by Sumayyah Hussein

Illustrated by Eman Salem

Library and Archives Canada Cataloguing in Publication

Title: Esa & Sol's adventures : the hunt for the Saphaea / written by Asma Maryam Ali ; edited by

Sumayyah Hussein ; illustrated by Eman Salem.

Other titles: Esa and Sol's adventures | Hunt for the Saphaea

Names: Ali, Asma Maryam, 1981- author. | Salem, Eman, illustrator.

Identifiers: Canadiana 20190201649 | ISBN 9781988796031 (softcover)

Subjects: LCSH: Plot-your-own stories. | LCGFT: Choose-your-own stories.

Classification: LCC PS8601.L525 E83 2019 | DDC jC813/.6—dc23

Compass Books appreciates the support of the
Ontario Arts Council

ONTARIO ARTS COUNCIL
CONSEIL DES ARTS DE L'ONTARIO

an Ontario government agency
un organisme du gouvernement de l'Ontario

*To Shifaa, Sanaa and Noah, my lights.
May the world always meet you with
love and respect.*

*For this book and every good thing
in my life, thank you to my beautiful
parents. And thank you to Dr. Shari
Golberg and Dr. Mubdi Rahman for your
guidance and support. And to my sister,
my pillar. And to Tariq Mahmood, who
paved the way for myself and countless
others to experience the magnificence
of Spain.*

Asma Maryam Ali

PROLOGUE

The year is 1080 in Cordoba, Spain. People of different religions and ethnicities live side by side in Spain under Muslim rule, studying together and coming up with brilliant new discoveries. They are developing new inventions and translating ancient texts. The work they do will eventually lead Europe into the Renaissance, a period of learning and progress for European societies.

One astronomer, Zarkali, has spent years of his life developing a particular instrument, the astrolabe, which he has named the Saphaea. His actual name is Abu Ishaq Ibrahim Ibn Yahya Al-Zarkali. He is also known as Arzachel.

While these are real facts, the two boys you will now meet are fictional, as is the story of their hunt.

Help them find the missing Saphaea!

"Come back, Abby!" screams Esa as he doubles over, panting.

"Not that waaayyyy!" yells Sol. His face turns pale as he watches his father's donkey gallop into the distance with the cart carrying all the juicy oranges they'd harvested that week.

"What will Isaiah say?" scolds Sol's aunt Miriam from the corner of the bustling market square. By now the two 9-year-old boys have become a spectacle for the entire square. Sol begins to run after Abby, but Esa jerks him back. "Sol, we gotta go. Zarkali told us to meet him at sunset by his workshop."

Suddenly, the image of the workshop pushes all thoughts of oranges from Sol's mind. The boys have waited months for this moment; Zarkali has a job for them. They abandon the orange stand and jet off, with angry elders waving fists at them for losing Isaiah's cart.

The boys scuff to a halt at Zarkali's door. Knock, knock, knock.

"We need to wait," whispers Esa to Sol, remembering the manners that Zarkali taught them. The boys sink down against the door and sit quietly on the doorstep. Sol rests his head on the wall while Esa smooths the dirt on the path with his hands.

Thoughts about the great scholar race through their minds. He was the most well-known astronomer in all of Spain. He never stopped reading and working and recording his findings, sometimes going without sleep for days. He was a perfectionist, and it showed in his work. His latest work was a brilliant astrolabe. The instrument was so detailed and precise that it could tell the height of mountains, the time of day and the position of stars in the sky. Day by day, the boys watched in awe as Zarkali worked on the instrument, and they wondered why such a great man would invite them into his workshop. They even hoped that, someday, he would ask them for help.

And now it seemed that today might be that wonderful day!

"Zarkali's worked patiently at his instruments all his life; 'course we can wait a bit for him," Sol says, interrupting the silence.

"I wonder how old he actually is?" says Esa, pensively.

"Probably a hundred," replies Sol. The boys wait several more minutes; it sounds like no one's inside.

Suddenly, they hear the thud of a heavy leather sandal on the doorstep beside them. The long wing of Zarkali's cloak sweeps past them as he unlocks the door and hurries into his workshop, causing them to fall backwards into the workshop with a bang. He and his assistant Aleho were out the whole time.

"It's gone! I've searched everywhere! It's gone!" Zarkali bellows at Aleho. The boys watch nervously as Zarkali, a tall, strong man, paces back and forth worriedly. The boys scurry to a corner of the dimly lit workshop.

"This can't be!" cries Aleho. "Have you tried—"

Zarkali interrupts him. "I've checked in every workshop from here to the **Mezquita**. IT'S LOST!!"

Zarkali notices the boys and turns towards them. "Why are you here at this hour, boys? It's almost dark out."

Esa replies in an almost-whisper, "You asked us here, sir." He shivers with fear at the sight of an angry Zarkali. Esa has never seen him angry before.

Glossary

Mezquita = "mosque" in Spanish. It refers to the Great Mosque of Cordoba, established by Abdul Rahman I in 784 A.D. Later on, it was converted to a Catholic cathedral. Despite the change, local Cordobans of all faiths have continued to call it "Mezquita" until today. The site is still in Cordoba and is visited by thousands of tourists every day

Zarkali begins, "I was going to ask you to deliver a package for me—"

"These two boys?!" Aleho interrupts, surprised.

"NO ONE WOULD NOTICE THEM," answers Zarkali angrily, ending any further questions from Aleho.

"But now," Zarkali sighs as he walks over to the window and looks out at the moon, "it's gone."

The boys' hearts sink with disappointment as they realize that their long-anticipated job is over. Squirming in his chair in the corner, Esa slowly asks, "W-What was it, sir?"

A lone tear gathers at one corner of Zarkali's glistening eyes, his silvery beard framing his bright face. "The Saphaea."

The boys' eyes widen with shock as Zarkali's words echo through the workshop.

The Saphaea.

Saphaea.

Saphaea.

Zarkali's astrolabe! His life's masterpiece!

"It's gone," whispers Zarkali as he lowers his head.

A loud knock breaks the deafening silence in the room. It's Isaiah, Sol's father, with Abby and an empty cart. He's come straight to Zarkali's workshop after finding Abby, knowing that his son would be there.

He stands in the doorway with a stern look on his face and glares at Sol and Esa. Knowing the trouble they're in for losing Abby, the boys silently march outside and climb into the cart. Their minds are full of the evening's events.

Whispering so that no one can overhear him, Esa leans over and says, "Sol, we have to find the Saphaea."

Glossary

Mezquita = "mosque" in Spanish. It refers to the Great Mosque of Cordoba, established by Abdul Rahman I in 784 A.D. Later on, it was converted to a Catholic cathedral. Despite the change, local Cordobans of all faiths have continued to call it "Mezquita" until today. The site is still in Cordoba and is visited by thousands of tourists every day

Interesting Facts

"Esa" is the Arabic version of the name "Jesus." Many Muslims are named "Esa" because Muslims also believe in Jesus Christ.

If Sol and Esa are stuck shovelling manure on the Isaiah farm at sunrise, turn to page 7.

If Sol and Esa head to town at sunrise, turn to page 9.

Scoop, scoop. scoop, scoop. The blades of two shovels hit manure and dump it into Isaiah's wagon in a dimly lit barn before sunrise. Sol and Esa were told they'd be doing this all day as a consequence for losing Abby the day before. Isaiah spoke to Esa's parents, Sumaiya and Ahmad, and they agreed on the spot.

Sol scolds his donkey. "I told you to stay put, Abby. All we had to do was sell the oranges in the market. I tell you stay, you go. I tell you go, you stay."

Abby suddenly neighs with fright and gallops out of the barn and toward the field. The boys drop the shovels and chase after her. Before they reach the field, they nearly run into a hooded figure standing under a tree at the edge of the orchard.

They look up, gasping for breath, and see an aged woman with brilliant bronze skin and piercing eyes. She's covered from head to toe and her white cloak hangs loosely around her. "Listen, my children," she whispers coarsely. "I am Munira. Welcome to the realm of the Known and Unknown."

"What!" cries Esa, slowly backing away from her.

"You must come with me," she continues.

"Bu —" Esa interrupts.

"If you do not," she raises her voice to a screech, "Your families will be in grave danger."

She glares at the shocked boys and stretches her hands out to grab them.

If the boys run back to the family farms, turn to page 10.

If Munira captures the boys, turn to page 11.

Esa's eyes are fixated on his father Ahmad's prayer beads, which must be completed before anyone stands up after the dawn prayer. Three more, two more, then one more bead.

Esa jumps up and runs out the door, slamming it behind him.

He wanders out into the darkness, looking over at the neighbouring farm where Sol and his family live. He paces back and forth while he waits for Sol to emerge with Abby. They've decided to ride her back to town to find the Saphaea.

He hears a whisper as Sol emerges. "Abby's too small for us both, Esa. Let's take turns. You first."

"Okay then," replies Esa as he prepares to mount Abby. Sol holds his hands together to give Esa a boost, and Esa raises his foot to get on.

If Abby kicks Esa, turn to page 14.

If the boys make it to town, turn to page 16.

The boys barely escape Munira's grip. They back away, zip around, and run as fast as they can back to their farms. What if their families are in danger?

"Mom! Dad!" Esa screams, terrified. He can hear Sol yelling for his parents at their house, too.

As Esa approaches his house, he notices that his front door is wide open as if someone had left in a hurry. He gasps, and his heart starts pounding.

He scurries from room to room and discovers that no one's there. Back outside, he spots the wagon and realizes that his parents and sisters couldn't have left.

The Isaiah farm. Maybe they've gone there.

But when Esa arrives, no one's around. Not even Sol.

The old woman is standing in the doorway of Sol's house.

"It's too late," she says. "They're all gone."

THE END

Munira grabs the boys by their collars and, with the strength of two men, pulls them into her cart.

"Let's go!" She scowls back at them as she whips her horse to speed up.

"W-Why us!?" Esa asks.

"My dad, my mom!" cries Sol.

"Come with me and you'll see," she snaps back as she fixes her gaze on the road ahead of her.

"Who are you, Munira?" asks Sol as he holds on for dear life.

"My father was Muhammad the Third, a great **Caliph**, and he left me his palace and treasures. I use them to teach women of all sorts. I read poems, and I compete with men in completing the uncompleted ones!"

"The uncompleted ones?" Esa asks.

"Yes, the uncompleted poems are a part of the mystical Realm of the Known and Unknown. "I know them!"

Glossary
Caliph = the traditional name given to the head of an Islamic state

The boys sit back in silent contemplation of this strange woman as she hurriedly drives them toward town. She stops just outside the town at Yehuda's apothecary. Yehuda is a renowned physician and an expert in interpreting the Torah, the holy book of the Jews. She jumps off with great agility and knocks at the door. Esa peeks in and notices a group of elders standing in a circle. They seem to be discussing an important matter, though what, he can't tell. He spots Zaynab, the master calligrapher, Ibn Taymur, the mathematician, and Yehuda himself. Is this some kind of order? Esa wonders.

Interesting Facts

The character Yehuda is named after Rabbi Yehuda Halevi of Cordoba who lived in the 11th and 12th centuries. He was a renowned physician, philosopher and poet. He wrote his poems in Hebrew and Arabic. To this day, he is the most revered Hebrew poet of his time.

The character of Munira is based on a real person, Wadallah, the daughter of the caliph Muhammad III of Cordoba. She died in the year 1091, in the time period of this story. Because he had no other children, she inherited his palaces and buildings and she built a literary hall where she educated women.

If the boys wait to see what will happen, turn to page 17.

If the boys jump off the cart and run for their lives, turn to page 18.

"AAAAGH!!" screams Esa as he falls to the floor writhing in pain. All he knows is that Abby had raised her hind leg and kicked him. Must've been for losing her the day before, he thinks to himself as the world around him starts spinning and he blacks out. He can't even see Sol anymore.

Esa wakes up hours later in his own bed with his mother, Sumaiya, tending to his bruises.

Ahmad, his father, is standing above him whispering prayers for his health in Arabic. Esa spots Isaiah doing the same in Hebrew at the far corner of the room with a worried expression on his face.

Esa turns to his mother.

"Mom," he whispers. "This is what I get for taking off."

"Yes, Esa," Sumaiya replies gently, "but it gets worse." She furrows her brow and looks over at Isaiah. She continues with a quivering voice, "Sol is missing."

Esa sits up and tries to bolt out of bed, but the pain of his bruises stops him. Sol, his best friend, is missing.

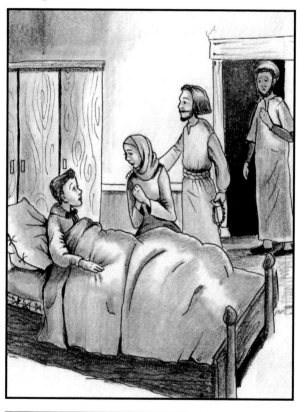

If Esa leaves with Isaiah to find Sol, turn to page 20.

If someone drops a clue off for Esa, turn to page 22.

Sol and Esa take turns riding Abby into town. Just before they get to Zarkali's workshop, Abby stops moving.

Sol whispers in the quiet of the morning and gives her a gentle kick, "Go on, girl!" But she refuses to move.

Sol jumps off, and he and Esa look her over carefully. Nothing appears to be wrong, but Abby seems anxious. Abby leans towards Sol and nudges him away from the workshop and toward a dark lane, almost knocking him over. Sol scratches his head, puzzled at Abby's behaviour.

"WHAT ARE YOU DOING, BOYS?" The boys whip their heads around to find a tall, heavy set soldier standing over them. "Don't you know there are thieves about the town?!" the soldier thunders. The boys have never seen this soldier in town, and his robes and sandals look odd to them.

They shake with fear at the sight of this strange man and look left and right for an escape.

If the boys are rescued, turn to page 37.

If the soldier completes his mission, turn to page 24.

The door of Yehuda's apothecary slowly opens, and Munira whispers several words to Zaynab, the master calligrapher. Zaynab looks over at the boys, who shrink back into the cart.

"Come in, boys," says Zaynab, opening her arms in welcome.

Too curious to leave such a special meeting, the boys get off the cart and walk behind the elders into the apothecary.

The elders encircle them, and Yehuda steps forward. "Boys, the day has come. You must deliver the Saphaea."

"It's m-missing!" the boys stammer in unison.

"No," Yehuda calmly replies. "It's here." Yehuda opens a leather sack that's hanging from his shoulder, reaches his hand in, and pulls out a golden circular object: the Saphaea. The boys' eyes widen with amazement. "We took it from Zarkali's workshop for safekeeping. There are thieves hunting for it. And now you must return it to him."

Turn to page 28.

The door of Yehuda's apothecary opens for Munira, and Zaynab, the master calligrapher, steps out to whisper to Munira. The boys scramble off Munira's cart and run as fast as they can down the lane.

Munira yells, "Come back!" as she chases them. She catches up to them with a speed faster than the best athletes in town. She almost grabs their collars again, but they jump a wall and continue running; she can't seem to make it over.

The boys pant their way through a conversation as they continue in the same direction, both knowing that they're headed towards the **Mezquita** for safety.

"Sol, I think Munira may be the one who took the Saphaea," exclaims Esa.

"Can't be!" retorts Sol, trying to catch up to Esa. "Why would you think that?"

"Think about it, Sol," Esa replies. "The morning after the Saphaea disappears, a scary lady appears to us out of nowhere, kidnaps us, and chases us down like she's on the hunt. If Zarkali wanted us to go with her, he would have told us."

"Wow, Esa," exclaims Sol, "I think you're right!" Suddenly, Sol hears a bam. Esa is sprawled on the floor; he has just run into a wall.

Esa sees the world around him spinning, then going black.

Glossary
Mezquita = "mosque" in Spanish. It is the nickname that was given by all Cordobans to the Great Mosque of Cordoba, established by Abdul Rahman I in 784 A.D.

Although the building is now used as a cathedral, most Cordobans today call it "Mezquita"

Interesting Facts
The character of Munira is based on a real person, Wadallah, the daughter of the caliph Muhammad III of Cordoba. She died in the year 1091, in the time period of this story. Because he had no other children, she inherited his palaces and buildings and she built a literary hall where she educated women and read poetry.

If the boys get help from an old friend, turn to page 37.

If the boys try to find their way into the Mezquita, turn to page 30.

"E-E-Esa," Isaiah stutters as he walks over to Esa in his bed, "can you come with me to find Sol? You know all of your favourite places."

"Yes, Sir," Esa replies glumly. *What a mess we've gotten into.*

An hour later, Esa is sitting with Isaiah in a small cart. Sol's mother Sarah has applied some medicine to his wounds and bandaged him up. Isaiah looks around frantically while Esa groans and winces in pain as they ride into town.

They stop at Zarkali's workshop, but it's shut up tight and the blinds are down, so they can't even peek in. They knock several times, but there's no answer. Just as they're about to leave, Zarkali's falcon, Abdul Rahman, swoops in as if he'll go right through the window. He collides into the closed window and bounces off, dropping a tiny leaflet into Esa's hands. Isaiah tends to a startled Abdul Rahman while Esa reads the Arabic script on the leaflet. There's only one line: "The boy is at the source."

As Esa reads it out loud, Isaiah stops cold, and his arms go limp. It must be my boy, Sol.

"What's the source, Sir?" asks Esa.

"It must be the **synagogue**. That's our sanctuary and the source of Jewish teachings and life."

"What about a river?" Esa replies. "It could be the biggest river around, the Wadi-Al-Kabir!"

Glossary
Synagogue = A synagogue is the Jewish place of worship

Interesting Facts
The Wadi-Al-Kabir is an Arabic word that means "big river." It describes a river that runs through Southern Spain. It is now called Guadalquivir, based on the Arabic name.

If they go to the Synagogue, turn to page 32.

If they go to the Wadi-Al-Kabir, turn to page 35.

Sumaiya, Esa's mother, forces him to stay in bed all day to recover from Abby's kick. He knows that it's also a punishment for the misadventures he and Sol got into. All Esa can think about is Sol. He and Sol were born in the same year in these neighbouring farms. They grew up together playing games, teasing their sisters, and getting into mischief. They shared stories and teachings and had meals together each week.

I can't lose Sol, Esa thinks to himself.

Later that day, when Esa's mother takes some soup to comfort Sol's worried mother, Sarah, Esa sneaks out of bed. He peeks out of his room to check if the coast is clear. His plan is to go out looking for clues about where Sol could be.

Knock, knock, knock.

Esa jumps with fright at the unexpected sound; who could be calling at this time of day? Esa runs to the front of the house and looks out the window, but no one's there. He runs to the door and opens it slightly, then notices a shiny key on the doorstep. He grabs it and shuts the door quickly.

What could this be for? Who left it? It must be a clue to Sol's whereabouts.

If Esa takes the key to Zarkali's workshop,
turn to page 73.

If Esa goes looking for a door that the key might fit,
turn to page 64.

The soldier takes the boys towards the guard house beside the Al-Modawar Gate to the west of the city. "I told you," he yells at the boys, "it's not safe here!"

But the boys get the eerie feeling that the soldier may not be safe either; he looks so strange.

The boys suddenly spot Zarkali leaving the mosque. For the first time ever, Zarkali's face is covered, but the boys recognize Zarkali's large, deep-set eyes. Esa tries to call out to him, but he doesn't seem to hear even though he's within earshot. All he's doing is talking to the man beside him about a scroll. Scroll? Sol wonders. The Saphaea is missing and he wants a scroll? Zarkali completely bypasses the distressed boys. He keeps his gaze fixed to the ground as he turns a corner and disappears.

As the soldier approaches the fort with the boys in tow, he stops at a wooden shed on the road and kicks the door open, causing the door to fall off its hinges and down to the ground.

Esa and Sol manage to pull their heads up to look around the room, and there, sitting calmly in the corner drinking tea, is Zarkali.

"Thank you, Battuta," says Zarkali, placing a white tea cup with blue flowers and a gold rim down on a matching saucer. The boys are too stunned to speak. How did Zarkali know the soldier? Battuta? He must not be a soldier after all!

Turning to the new arrivals, Zarkali states calmly, "Boys, we're going to the ruins of Madinat-az-Zahra." The boys' hearts almost leap out of their chests. No one, not even the worst criminal, dares go to Madinat-az-Zahra. It was sacked during the civil wars, and it's always the subject of stories about hauntings, disappearances and strange creatures turning up there.

But Zarkali stands up, hurries out of the shed, and yells, "LET'S GO!"

The group rides for an hour and arrives at Madinat-az-Zahra with Battuta leading the way. It was once a splendid city built by Abdul Rahman III, who declared himself **Caliph** at the time. He wanted it to be a wonder for all the world, and it was. Remarkable inventions were passed on to Europe through this special place, and customs like three-course meals were invented and passed on, too. Through it, Spain made its mark as the height of culture and civilization in the world.

The boys gasp at the sight of it. Tall columns and buildings abound with stunning carvings and paintings on the walls and pillars. Strange holes line the beautiful creations where jewels once were; they were looted during the civil wars. It's said that there were gold and jewels everywhere in the city. The remnants of all sorts of structures are spread about; baths and markets and homes and stables. And in the centre, a magnificent palace with steps leading up to the façade where the private quarters of the Caliph were. The whole thing is in ruins, but it's still a magnificent sight to behold.

Glossary
Caliph = the traditional name given to the head of an Islamic state

Interesting Facts
The character Battuta is named after the famous scholar Ibn Battuta who travelled across the Medieval world and recorded stories about the places he saw.
Madinat-az-Zahra was an actual wonder city built by Abdul Rahman III. It is now in ruins and has been declared a UNESCO World Heritage Site.

If the group is chased at the ruins, turn to page 66.

If the group come across a human skeleton, turn to page 69.

Esa and Sol are ecstatic at being entrusted with the Saphaea. Yehuda hands it to them and says, mysteriously, "The Saphaea is only the beginning. You, Esa and Sol, must see this quest through to the end."

"What's the end, Sir?" asks Sol.

Yehuda replies, "The scrolls—"

Munira interrupts with a shout, "You've said too much!"

Yehuda suddenly backs away and covers his mouth.

Munira steps in. "Boys, take this to the port of Tarifa and meet Zarkali. Give it to him."

She packs the boys into a cart headed to the port of Tarifa, a town on the Mediterranean Sea. The cart is filled with goods to be shipped to Morocco.

"Off you go, and don't turn back," she says sternly, as if her mission is complete. The boys watch the apothecary and elders fade into the distance as the cart clinks and rattles its way to Tarifa.

If Zarkali takes the astrolabe from the boys,
turn to page 38.

If Zarkali leaves with them to Morocco, turn to page 40.

Sol and Esa run along the wall of the **Mezquita**, frantically searching for a way in. They come across a beaten-up wooden door that suddenly swings open. They jump through the doorway, and find themselves tumbling down a set of stairs. They crash in a heap at the bottom while the door shuts tightly behind them. Worn out and bruised, they lie at the bottom of the stairs for a few minutes before staggering to their feet. They look around; they're in a dark room full of old books, scrolls, and cobwebs. They've fallen into some kind of cellar beneath the **Mezquita**.

Pushing their way past mounds of cobwebs and nearly tripping over each other as a rat scurries by, the boys come upon another staircase. This one is quite narrow and it's been beautifully decorated. Some Arabic script is painted onto the tiles that line the outside of the staircase. It reads:

❉

"FOR THOSE WHO REACH THE CELLAR, BEWARE,

FOR THEY WILL FIND THE NORTH STAR HERE,

A WAY TO UPLIFT,

A PLACE TO FALL,

THIS JOURNEY IS FOR ONE, BUT NOT FOR ALL."

❉

Esa turns to Sol. "This is a clue! What do you think it could mean?"

Turn to page 42.

Isaiah and Esa knock on the large **synagogue** doors and wait in the hot midday sun for any kind of answer. The **synagogue** closes at **siesta**, but Isaiah hopes that someone will let him in under the circumstances.

"The boy is at the source. This must be the source," Isaiah repeats over and over as he paces back and forth.

So quietly that they barely notice it, one of the two doors slowly opens. Isaiah and Esa sneak in as fast as they can to catch whoever opened it. But it's only the janitor, an elderly lady with long silvery hair and wide green eyes. She's dressed in dirty rags.

"Qasmuna, is **Rabbi** Jonah in?" asks Isaiah.

Glossary
Rabbi = a Jewish scholar or religious leader
Siesta = traditionally, a nap that Muslims had after the midday prayer, which the people of Spain built into their day

Interesting Facts
In Medieval Times, many Jews established thriving societies in Spain. One of those was in Cordoba, where they lived and worked closely under the rule of Muslim caliphs. This period in Jewish history is often called the "Golden Age." Jews in Spain were known as "Sephardim" and are still called that today.

The character Qasmuna is named after the renowned Female Jewish Arabic-language poet Qasmuna bint Isma'il who lived in Spain in the 12th century. Only three of her poems have been passed on until today.

"No, and he won't be back today," she replies.

Tears well up in Isaiah's eyes, and he holds his hands out in prayer.

Qasmuna lets him finish then gently says, "Come tell me your troubles, Isaiah." Feeling helpless, Isaiah follows Qasmuna towards what appears to be her tiny closet full of brooms and buckets. Esa is close behind them.

They enter through a small, crooked door and stop in astonishment, gazing around the room. It's a large room with a high ceiling and walls painted in a beautiful emerald hue. Two walls are lined with shelves, floor to ceiling, and each shelf is packed with books of every size, shape, and colour. Candles are spread around the room, and all of them are lighted, giving the room a warm, uplifting feel. Several desks are against the other walls, and Esa can see rocks holding down old parchment and leather with Hebrew on some and Arabic on others.

Qasmuna leaves the room and returns soon after carrying tea. "Sit down, Isaiah. Who's your friend?"

"This is Esa," Isaiah replies. "Wh-What is this place?"

"This is my little space, Isaiah," Qasmuna replies in her high-pitched, creaky voice. I read and study. I help **Rabbi** with translations. I share ancient wisdom with visiting scholars and rabbis. Now, I will help you."

"We can't find Sol," Isaiah says with a quiver in his voice.

Qasmuna stands up immediately, as if she was waiting for those words. "Come with me, my son," Qasmuna says, motioning Isaiah towards a bookshelf.

Isaiah and Esa turn to one another, confused. She wants them to walk into a wall.

Turn to page 45.

With the tiny scroll in hand, Isaiah and Esa head to the river, Wadi-Al-Kabir. The shores are quiet and peaceful in spots, and busy and full of people in other spots. Traders and goods and donkeys with carts are everywhere. The air is filled with the smell of fish and spices. Finding Sol will be like looking for needle in a haystack. Isaiah and Sol stand before it all, looking up into the sky at a giant flock of seagulls.

Suddenly, a man holding a knife jumps in front of Isaiah. Isaiah pushes Esa behind him, out of harm's way.

"What do you want?!" Isaiah yells, moving backward and pushing Esa back too.

Without saying a word, the strange man slowly pulls out a finely carved piece of wood from behind his back. Isaiah and Esa breathe sighs of relief as they realize that the man is working on the leg of a beautifully crafted armchair.

"This is about what you want," the stranger replies mysteriously in a monotone. "You're looking for your boy, aren't you?"

"How do you know that?!" Isaiah asks angrily. The suspense is too much for him.

"I've hidden him in my best cabinet, and I have him on that ship there," replies the man with a slight grin, motioning his head toward a massive ship being loaded with wooden furniture.

Isaiah grabs the man by the arms, "what?! give him to me!"

"Take it easy," the stranger says calmly, shaking the leg of the armchair toward Isaiah. Isaiah backs down. "Come with me and I'll show him to you."

Without saying a word, Isaiah pushes Esa farther back and says, "You stay here." Isaiah follows the man to the ship, and Esa watches them disappear into the crowd.

If Esa follows the man and Isaiah to the ship,
turn to page 48.

If Isaiah and Esa are separated on the docks,
turn to page 50.

Suddenly, the boys feel a sharp tug at their collars as someone pulls them back and jerks them in the direction of a nearby shop. They spin around to find Aleho, Zarkali's assistant. The boys follow him into the shop, and he locks the door behind them.

"Boys, I'm here to rescue you!"

"Help us!" cries Esa, exasperated.

"I will definitely help you, boys," says Aleho with a grin on his face that seems half-friendly and half-dangerous.

Aleho helps the boys dust themselves off. "I was sent to get you. And now I need to give you a clue."

"What is—" Sol starts to ask Aleho. But his question is interrupted by the sound of the tall soldier shouting Aleho's name. Who is this man and what does he want with Aleho?

"Come here Aleho!" the soldier yells.

The soldier bangs at the door until the old hinges fall off the wall and, bam, the door falls flat into the room, revealing Aleho and the boys.

"THIEF!" yells the soldier. The boys are shocked. Aleho can't be the thief.

Turn to page 52.

After two days of bumpy travels over the rolling hills of Southern Spain, the boys arrive at the busy port of Tarifa.

The driver, a kind man who seems to know the elders from Yehuda's apothecary, tells them to wait in his cart just outside a small library.

Zarkali suddenly appears in front of the cart, smiling from ear to ear.

"You did it, boys," he bellows with delight. He hugs the boys and pulls them off the cart.

"I asked the elders to keep the Saphaea for me. It was never stolen! But now that you have done this job, you are in danger. You must go to the town of **Granada** immediately."

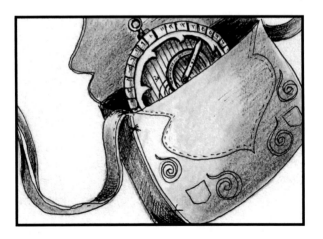

Zarkali swiftly grabs the leather sack carrying the Saphaea out of Esa's hands and motions the boys back to the cart.

Shocked at Zarkali's statement and afraid for their lives, the boys back out into the street and Zarkali hurries back into the library with the sack.

Glossary
Granada = a town in Southern Spain and the site of the last Muslim kingdom that existed before the Catholic conquest of Spain

If the boys follow Zarkali, turn to page 55.

If the boys go to Granada, turn to page 53.

Esa and Sol meet Zarkali at the busy port of Tarifa. Zarkali looks worn out and worried. He tells Esa and Sol that he had to give the Saphaea to the elders for safekeeping and that he knew they had it all along. Then, the elders had to get it to the boys to bring to Zarkali in Tarifa.

Zarkali and the boys board a ship travelling across the Mediterranean Sea to Morocco. Eventually, they arrive at Tangiers, a port on the northern tip of Morocco, filled with travellers from all around the world. Tradespeople bustle about, pushing their way through crowds with wagons in tow. Some of them have stalls with goods and are bargaining with travellers and tradespeople.

The boys, stunned at the sights and sounds, follow Zarkali as he hurries in one direction on the pier. He seems to know the port well.

Finally, they arrive at the end of the pier and come to a halt. A row of tall Berber men and women, all dressed in similar garments, jewelry and sandals, tower in front of the boys. The Berbers are the indigenous people of Morocco and are respected for their ancient knowledge and traditions. Zarkali opens his arms and walks into a big hug with the men, then nods at the women respectfully. He seems to know them pretty well.

"Here are Esa and Sol!" he bellows. Esa and Sol freeze, shocked that the group seems to be expecting them.

A Berber woman steps forward. "Welcome, boys. We have been waiting for you." She grabs the leather sack with the Saphaea and throws it into the sea. The boys gasp and look at Zarkali, who does nothing.

"In fact," she continues, "the Saphaea means nothing to us. Zarkali's job was to bring YOU to us. And he has succeeded. You belong to us now."

THE END

Interesting Facts
The mother of the first leader of the Muslims in Spain, Abdul Rahman I, was an indigenous Berber woman from Northern Africa.

"Esa, you find the North Star with an astrolabe," Sol exclaims excitedly. "Maybe it's a clue to the Saphaea!"

"But where?" Esa scratches his head. "A way to uplift, a place to fall?"

The boys walk around the beautifully decorated staircase. Esa suddenly jumps. "This is the mimbar of our mosque!

"What's a mimbar?" Sol asks.

"It's a narrow staircase that the prayer leader stands on when giving his sermon so all the worshippers can see him. It's supposed to be on the ground level, but these stairs start on the ground floor and continue through a passageway down to the cellar! How unusual!"

The boys' hearts race as they examine the mimbar. "Sol," Esa adds, "stairs are a way to uplift and a place to fall! The Saphaea must be here!"

The boys scramble up and down the mimbar stairs, frightening all sorts of bugs and moths and kicking up dust left and right. They begin pulling at it for loose boards. Sol finds one on the third stair from the bottom and peeks inside. There, he sees a clean white cloth wrapped around something. It's sitting in a pile of cobwebs and bug skeletons.

Sol bravely reaches his hand in to pull out the cloth, but it's much too heavy to do on his own. Esa scurries down beside him and reaches his arms in, too. They heave it out together. The cloth looks new. With pounding hearts and shaking hands, they quickly unfold the cloth. There, before them, is not one, but three newly-made astrolabes, the likes of which they've never seen before, and none of them is the Saphaea.

"Ahhhhh" they gasp with excitement and intrigue. This is a treasure for Zarkali.

They must get the astrolabes to him immediately. They find old rags and wrap the astrolabes in them. No one must think they're carrying something valuable.

They scurry up the cellar stairs and push the door hard, causing them to fall down on the stairs and the astrolabes to go crashing down. The door is jammed!

Both boys pick themselves up and head back to the door, banging on it and pushing it, hitting it with anything they can find. It's locked. They scramble around the room searching for another door or window, but there's nothing to be found.

They're trapped, and there's no way out.

THE END

Isaiah and Esa creep behind Qasmuna and watch her pull a book from a shelf on the wall.

Ah, she's going to give us some advice, they think to themselves.

But the book doesn't leave the shelf. Instead, the shelf moves back into the wall with a thundering sweep. Esa and Isaiah gasp in surprise and take a quick step back while Qasmuna slips into the gap as fast as she can. "COME QUICK!" she screams at the top of her voice. Thinking that this may be his only chance to find Sol, Isaiah grabs Esa and pushes through the gap just before the door closes.

There, sitting against the wall of a narrow passage on the other side, wrapped up in a blanket and eating an orange, is Sol.

Isaiah falls to his knees in shock. He opens his arms, and Sol runs into them. "My boy," cries Isaiah, letting out the sobs that he's been holding back.

Qasmuna steps behind Isaiah and gently places her hand on his shoulder. "Isaiah," she says in a desolate tone. "This, is the end."

Isaiah slowly turns his head to face her, tears streaming down his face. "What?!"

"When the boys began searching for the astrolabe," Qasmuna continues, "they entered the realm of the Known and Unknown. This is a realm of ancient secrets, and the people who seek them belong to the Known and Unknown Order. It's an honour to be a part of the order, but it means that the lives of the seekers will forever be in danger, for there are many who want to know, but don't deserve it, and who want to steal secrets from the seekers. I belong to the order, and thankfully I'm still alive, but I disguise my identity here in the **synagogue**. Now, Esa and Sol belong to the order, and they're being hunted for it. I'm afraid I can't let them back into the town."

Glossary

Synagogue = A synagogue is the Jewish place of worship

Isaiah, Esa, and Sol are dumbfounded. Qasmuna lifts her right arm and points her finger down a small dark passageway. "There," she says firmly, glaring at them. "A series of tunnels that lead out of Cordoba. Take them to safety and never come back."

"But—" Isaiah begins.

"Never come back!" Qasmuna interrupts. She hands them a lighted torch and some bread, cheese, and water wrapped up in cloth and waves as they scurry down the passageway and out of sight.

THE END

Esa follows Isaiah and the strange man with the knife all the way to the ship. From time to time, Isaiah looks back to check to see if Esa is where he left him. His heart sinks when he realizes that Esa is gone, too. Esa dodges out of sight each time and then scurries to catch up, almost tripping over a stray dog and knocking down a barrel of lemons.

Finally, Isaiah and the man make it to the ship, with Esa close behind. Esa barely makes it on board before the gangway is pulled up. The man leads Isaiah down to the bay and stops. Isaiah's eyes pop. There before them, stretching from one side of the ship to the other, are dozens of the most magnificent wardrobes that he's ever seen, with brilliant colours, gold embellishments, and exquisite paintings. He stands in awe for a second or two, then begins to wonder which one Sol may be in. He takes a step toward them.

"Stop," says the strange man sternly, extending his arm in front of Isaiah. "We're waiting for someone."

Isaiah breathes a sigh of relief. It must be Sol.

They hear the footsteps of a young boy approaching and turn around. It's Esa.

"I've been waiting for you," says man in his odd, monotonous tone. "I knew you'd follow us."

Isaiah looks at the man and Esa, shocked. He has so many questions, but he can't seem to utter a word.

"Now," continues the man, "I've got a surprise for you. There's no Sol on this ship. This ship is going to Bordeaux, in France, and you are going to sell my wardrobes for me! You will not be back for six months."

THE END

Esa runs back and forth on the riverbank, struggling to see Isaiah and the strange man. From time to time, they disappear, then reappear, until they finally board the ship. The gangway goes up as soon as they board, and the ship sets off.

Esa panics. What can this mean? Won't he come back!

"They're not coming back, Esa," a voice whispers in his ear. Esa jumps and backs away from the voice, trips over a large rock, and falls to the ground. He looks up with terror and sees Maria, **Bishop** Josef's wife. She bends over to pick Esa up, hugging him as he realizes that more of his loved ones have gone missing. Esa silently cries on her shoulder. "Let me take you to safety, my child."

Esa quietly follows her onto her wagon, where **Bishop** Josef is sitting with a smile on his face. Doesn't the **Bishop** realize how awful this is?

"Come, boy," **Bishop** Josef says gently, "a cup of tea and a piece of bread will do you good."

Nothing will do me good, Esa thinks to himself.

Esa leans on Maria for comfort, and suddenly, something tickles him from behind. He jumps up giggling, and jerks himself away from Maria, almost falling off the wagon. When his laughter stops he sees two familiar eyes staring at him. They're Sol's.

Esa leaps forward to hug Sol, falling into some hay at the back of the wagon. "Sol! Where were you?? We've been looking everywhere for you!"

"I've been with **Bishop** Josef and Maria all this time." Sol replies. "We've been looking for you!"

"But Abby kicked me, and then you went missing, Sol!" Esa retorts.

Before the boys can sort it out, **Bishop** Josef interrupts with a yell. "We're taking you to safety in **Granada**! Cordoba is no longer safe for you, boys!" The boys look at each other with puzzled faces and then fall to each side of the wagon as Maria signals the horses to double their speed. The boys are bumped from side to side for hours. All they can manage to do is hold on for their lives.

Glossary

Bishop = a clergyman who is in charge of a group of churches and gives holy orders

Granada = a town in Southern Spain and the site of the last Muslim petty kingdom that existed before the Catholic conquest of Spain

Turn to page 53.

Aleho bolts out the door, forgetting about the boys and the clue. The boys join the soldier and run after him; this could be better than any clue.

"Thief! Thief! Thief!" they yell as they thunder through the narrow streets of Cordoba.

The boys nearly catch up to him by dodging peasants and carts. Just as they do, they come up to Zarkali's workshop, where a strange red flag is hanging on the door.

Perplexed, they slow down to a jog.

"Sol, let's find out what this means!" Esa yells out, signalling Sol to stop.

But Sol is determined. "If Aleho is the thief, he might have the astrolabe; we must catch him!"

If the boys stop at Zarkali's workshop, turn to page 75.

If the boys capture Aleho, turn to page 58.

The group finally arrives in **Granada**. The boys have only heard of **Granada** in stories. It's a rising kingdom full of beautiful buildings and talented craftsmen. People are discovering new things, and they practice different religions. It's said to be like Cordoba in its golden age.

But their families. *They may never see their families again.*

Just as that horrible thought sinks in, the wagon stops at an old house surrounded by olive trees. The boys shrink in fright. This doesn't look like **Granada**.

The boys are yelled at. "Get off!!" They leap up and off the wagon. With sweaty palms, they slowly walk toward the house and racing hearts. They're terrified.

As they approach the house, the front door eerily swings open for them to enter.

They walk in, and there before them are their families seated at large tables lavishly filled with piles of bread, fruit, meat, honey, and pastries. Everyone is laughing and joking and throwing frogs in the air.

Throwing frogs in the air?

"WAKE UP, MY BOY!!!" The voice of Ahmad, Esa's father, rings through Esa's head as Ahmad shakes Esa frantically. Esa lifts his pounding head off the ground and writhes in pain as his hand accidentally touches the place where Abby kicked him. He moans while several people around him sigh with relief. He manages to pry his eyes open to see Ahmad, Isaiah, Sol and his mother, Sumaiya, standing over him. Suddenly, Esa remembers the frogs, and the truth dawns on him.

It was only a dream.

THE END

Esa and Sol turn their questioning gaze from Zarkali to one another.

"What should we do, Esa?" asks Sol.

"We wait, of course!" Esa whispers excitedly.

"But you heard him! We're in danger. What if someone's after us?" Sol shouts, not noticing the people around them slowing down to look at these strange boys.

"But the elders said that we have to see this through to the end, Sol, and I know this isn't the end."

"Esa, we've delivered the astrolabe. Our job is done!" Sol exclaims with finality.

"Let's see," Esa says as he grabs Sol's arm and pulls him into a corner by the library door.

Esa and Sol watch from the corner by the library as Zarkali slowly opens the door, peeks outside, then bolts through the door, around the corner, and down a dark alley. The boys make sure they're out of his sight and then hurry behind him. He's headed for a large wagon driven by a hooded man and pulled by two horses. The boys catch up to him, almost stepping on his cloak, then come to a halt as he begins to climb on. They scurry under the wagon, but as the wheels begin to turn, they hurry out to the back, grab the ledge, and jump on. Esa nearly falls off, but Sol grabs his arm and pulls him up just in time. They quickly pull old furs onto themselves so that no one sees them.

Just then, Esa begins to sneeze. "My allergies!" he whispers to Sol, his voice quivering. Esa sneezes and sneezes until they're out of town and the other riders can hear the sneezes in the quiet of the countryside.

Al Zarkali turns around, reaches his hand underneath the furs, and before he sees their faces, he bellows, "Esa, Sol, come out! We're going back to Cordoba!"

The boys' heads pop up, their eyes as wide as the Saphaea. How did he know they were there?

"I knew you'd come!" exclaims a pleased Zarkali.

"You wanted us here, Sir?" asks Sol. "I thought you told us to get out of danger." .

"I wanted to see if you'd be brave enough to make it, boys, and you are! You'll see why! I am about to make my greatest discovery."

The boys' ears perk up with wonder. What could be his greatest discovery?

"Sir," Esa asks meekly, "I-isn't the Saphaea your greatest discovery?"

Just then, the wagon comes to a halt in front of three cliffs with a passage between the first and second. The foremost edges of each cliff could make the three points of a triangle.

Turn to page 61.

There's no telling what's in Zarkali's workshop, but if Aleho is the thief, he must know where the Saphaea is.

Esa and Sol pick up their pace again and run ahead of the soldier in pursuit of Aleho. They dodge past carts and bystanders until they catch up to Aleho. He looks like he's headed for the stable where Zarkali keeps his horse. They quickly run around to the back while Aleho darts inside, looking for the horse. They climb a ladder to a window in the hayloft and climb onto the hayloft watching Aleho pace back and forth. Zarkali must have his horse; there's nothing in the stable except some hay and an old shovel.

Aleho bites his fingernails and looks out the window. He knows the boys will catch up to him soon; he just doesn't know where they are. Just then, Esa and Sol pull a large dirty blanket to the edge of the hayloft and throw it on top of Aleho, covering him completely.

"Aaaaaagghhh!!" he screams. He wriggles around, sneezing and coughing, trying to free himself. Just then, a sack falls out of his jacket and drops to the floor with a clang. The boys spot the shiny engraved surface of the Saphaea peeping out of the bag. They jump down, and Sol throws himself on top of Aleho, wrestling him while he kicks and punches into the air, unable to see because of the dust in his eyes. Esa grabs the Saphaea and runs to a corner of the barn.

Bang.

The soldier comes crashing through the stable door followed by an angry mob of townspeople. They heard Aleho's scream and knew he was inside.

"IT'S OVER, ALEHO!" yells the soldier. He takes the Saphea from Esa then pushes Sol aside to grab Aleho's arms.

"Explain yourself!" the soldier bellows.

"I-I-I couldn't help myself. I assisted Zarkali for years with that brilliant instrument. I have a right to know what it's for!"

"What it's for?!" Sol repeats. "It's for finding your direction, Aleho."

"No, boy!" Aleho shouts gruffly. "It's for so much more than that. Ancient treasures await the holder of the Saphaea."

Esa's and Sol's jaws drop open. Their minds race with questions.

"Well, for you, Aleho," replies the solider, "the only thing that awaits you is prison."

THE END

"The Saphaea is only a tool, my boys. I need it to find my greatest discovery yet!" Zarkali fixes his gaze on the boys. "I finished the Saphaea two nights ago, but I discovered that a thief was out to steal it from me at any cost. So, I told most people that I lost the Saphea and went into hiding for my safety."

The boys let out huge sighs of relief and drop their heads to their chests, their bodies suddenly going limp.

"But sir, what have we got to do with your quest?" Sol asks, lifting his head.

"Because what we find today, my children, is a trust that I must give to you." Esa and Sol turn to each other in speechless astonishment.

Zarkali takes out a map of the cliffs that they have come to. It has three caves and a passage marked on it in the same form that they see before them. He stands in the middle of the triangle and then takes out the Saphaea. The boys stare at Zarkali's hands.

"Now, this astrolabe will tell me where Jerusalem is. I'm looking for the cave in the same direction as that marvellous city." Zarkali uses a line engraved on the back of the Saphaea to find Jerusalem.

"There it is," says Zarkali as he points in one direction, lining his arm up with one of the caves. "And now," he shouts as delight and relief descend on his face in equal measure, "I have found the scrolls!" The cliffs echo his words, bouncing his voice off the mountains around them:

"The scrolls.

Scrolls.

Scrolls."

Scrolls. The word rings in the boys' heads. His greatest discovery is the scrolls.

They all run toward the cave and the hooded man holds a torch as Zarkali clears away sticks and cobwebs to make room to walk, then crawl, to the end of the cave. The boys peer in from the mouth of the cave and watch with delight as Zarkali reaches his long arm into a hole.

He slowly lifts his hand out, covered in a mess of leaves, cobwebs, and bird bones. He raises it up for the group to see. "These, he exclaims with excitement, "are the ancient **Salaam-Shalom scrolls**. And you, Esa and Sol, are now entrusted with them."

THE END

Glossary
Salaam = "peace" in Arabic
Shalom = "peace" in Hebrew

Interesting Facts
Jerusalem is a special place to many people, including Muslims, Christians and Jews.

In reality, there are no Salaam-Shalom scrolls. Use your imagination to think of what such scrolls might include!

Esa places the key in his pocket and races to his room for his hat and shoes. He double checks that no one's around to see him leave, then bolts out the door. There are several farmhouses in the area. Maybe the key is for a house or cellar where someone is holding Sol.

After trying the key in every door for miles, Esa sits down at the edge of the Isaiah farm and holds his head in his hands. What a mess. Sol's missing, the Saphaea's missing, and now his family must think that he's missing.

Wait, how come no one's come looking for me? he wonders to himself. What if everyone's missing?

Esa remembers that there's one door that he didn't try: his own. What if someone kidnapped his family, not just Sol? He runs back to his house and places the key in the lock. Sure enough, it clicks open, and he turns the knob, his heart about to jump out of his chest in fear.

As he opens the door, standing before him are his mother, sister, Sarah…and Sol.

"So you took the key we left you," Sumaiya chides him. "It was a test to see if you'd leave again against our orders, and you did! We found Sol while you were out looking for a lock to fit this key into," she says, grabbing the key from his hand.

"My boy, don't you see that if you'd listened, all would have been well? You must learn to listen to your parents. It's the key that fits all locks!"

THE END

The group wander up the steps of Madinat-az-Zahra to the throne room that overlooks the city. Four square pools sit side by side in front of it and together they make a large square. In the midday heat, the boys imagine taking a dive into one of them. But the imagining doesn't last long.

"Grrrrrrrrrr!" The group jumps and turns around in fright. There, before them, is a large wolf snarling at them. The boys grab hold of Zarkali, who pushes the boys behind him for safety. Several other wolves emerge from dark corners and creep toward them. This must be their territory now.

The group slowly backs away without realizing how close they are to the edge of one of the pools.

Splash.

Battuta, Zarkali, Esa and Sol all tumble into the water. As they make sense of what's happened to them, they swim backwards and further into the pools, towards the centre of the large square.

"Fast, boys! Wolves are good swimmers!" yells Zarkali.

They all swim as fast as they can, splashing anxiously in every direction. But as they glance back, they notice that the wolves aren't following them. Instead, the wolves are backing away with frightened expressions.

The group stops swimming when they get to the centre and hold onto each other, not sure what to expect next. They grasp the ledge of a fountain in the centre of the square, their feet pushing against the basin underneath the water, searching for some kind of ledge to rest on.

"Ok, boys—" Zarkali begins to plan their next move.

Just then, Sol's foot seems to slip, and he's pulled under the water instantly. Zarkali dips underneath to see what's happened. The basin is spreading apart into four sections, revealing a dark space underneath the fountain. Sol has disappeared inside of it, and now they're all being pulled in.

Completely blindsided, each of them feels himself being pulled further and further into a deep hole until they all fall into a pile on top of Zarkali on a beautiful marble floor.

When they come to, they look around in complete awe. It's a magnificent room with floral fragrances, mirror walls, splendid furniture lined with gold and jewels, and the most exquisite carpets that they've ever seen.

"The throne room," whispers Zarkali. "This is exactly like Abdul-Rahman III's throne room. This must be his, too, a hidden replica of the one above." They all stand up and walk around the room, silently gaping at the wondrous sights before them. As they approach the throne, the most shocking sight awaits them. It's a girl sitting comfortably eating some grapes.

She smiles at them and says, "I'm Zahra, and my great-great grandfather was Abdul-Rahman III. Welcome to my Kingdom."

THE END

Battuta leads the group to the ruins of Abdul-Rahman's private quarters. They're still gaping at the wondrous sights before them. Battuta seems to lead them through dozens of rooms, each one smaller than the last, until they get to a room the size of a closet. There, they find the complete skeleton of a person, with the skull against the wall, forehead first.

Battuta pushes the skeleton aside and it collapses to the floor in a large heap of bones. He places his finger on a stone in the bottom of the wall where the skeleton was sitting. "He must've been trying to find it, too."

The boys turn to one another questioningly: Find what? They ask one another with their glances.

Then, Battuta starts counting stones upwards. "One, two, three, four…" When he gets to eleven, he pushes the stone with all his might. It's remarkably loose, and suddenly, the whole wall shifts back, revealing some loose boards in the floor beneath the wall. The boys start shaking with nervousness while Zarkali walks right up to the wall and squats down, as if he expected the whole thing. The boys run up to him to see what he's doing. Battuta helps him to lift some floorboards, and they throw them aside.

"Yes!" bellows Zarkali. "Help me, Battuta." They lift out a large gold bowl that they can barely carry together and place it in the centre of the room.

Then, Battuta runs to the windows and opens them. He even opens a window in the ceiling. The boys are speechless. What can this mean?

"Boys, we don't need the Saphaea," says Zarkali calmly. The boys' eyes open wide in shock. Zarkali continues, "It was just a tool to tell us how to get to the scrolls." Scrolls. They'd heard him talking about scrolls. "But now, this bowl will show them to us."

A bowl? the boys wonder.

"This is the mercury bowl of Abdul-Rahman III," he explains as Battuta takes out a large vial from his coat and pours a strange substance into the bowl. "He would use it to impress his guests by pouring this, mercury, into it." Zarkali points to the strange substance. "When the sun hit it, it would light up the throne room and blind guests for a moment. He would use it to make himself seem like a wonder to them."

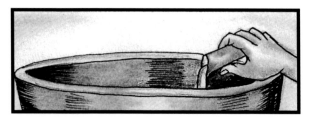

"Ahh," remark the boys in unison.

"But sir, you spent years working day and night on the Saphaea," Sol remarks. "Isn't it precious to you?"

"I did, my boy, but it was only a tool. The things we work on, the achievements we make, they're all tools to help us to achieve our true purpose, which is to serve. Once they no longer help us to serve, we no longer need them, like the Saphaea. Now, the bowl is the tool we need."

"But how will it help us find the scrolls?" Esa asks.

"Watch, boys," replies Zarkali. As the bowl is filled, the light in the room is magnified and stuns them all, leaving them struggling to see. Zarkali places his head out the window facing the mountains behind Madinat-az-Zahra, and the boys do the same.

Zarkali points to a cave on one mountainside. "There," he says.

"What is it, Sir?" Sol asks.

"See how that cave seems to be lighted up inside? That's the light of the mercury bowl."

"Wow!" the boys exclaim in wonder.

"And," Zarkali continues, "that's the cave where the scrolls are."

"What are the scrolls?" Esa asks.

"I'll show you. Let's go there now," Zarkali replies in a relieved whisper.

Zarkali, Esa, Sol, and Battuta climb up to the cave, and Battuta holds a torch as Zarkali clears away sticks and cobwebs to make room to walk, then crawl, to the end of the cave. The boys peer into the cave and watch with delight as Zarkali reaches the end of the cave and stretches his arm into a hole.

He slowly lifts his hand out, covered in a mess of leaves, cobwebs, and bird bones. He raises it up for the group to see. "These," he exclaims with excitement, "are the ancient **Salaam-Shalom scrolls**. And you, Esa and Sol, are now entrusted with them."

THE END

Glossary
Salaam = "peace" in Arabic
Shalom = "peace" in Hebrew

Interesting Facts
In reality, there are no Salaam-Shalom scrolls. You can use your imagination to think of what such scrolls might include!

Esa sneaks out of his house at noon and trudges all the way into town. He's doesn't want to risk being spotted if he rides an animal.

He scurries through the streets of Cordoba, dodging any familiar faces and avoiding all the places he visits often, which are many. Finally, he arrives at Zarkali's workshop and knocks on the door. He looks around and nervously inserts the key in the lock, then attempts to turn it, but it won't budge. Esa begins to panic. He tries to wriggle it out, shaking it, pushing it, and pulling it with all his might, but nothing happens. It seems to be the right key, but it's jammed.

"Psst!" Someone whispers at him from around the corner. He makes one more attempt to unjam the key, but it doesn't move. He leaves it in the door and hurries around the corner, but no one's there. He spots a blue shoe sticking out from a space between the back of Zarkali's workshop and the bakery behind it. Esa knows that shoe; it's Sol's!

He sneaks up to it and steps on Sol's foot.

"AAAAAAAGH!" Sol comes tumbling out and quickly slaps his hand over his mouth to silence himself.

"Sol! Where have you been?! I was so worried!"

"Esa," Sol whispers while he winces in pain. "When Abby kicked you this morning, a dark hooded figure rode up and dropped a scroll for me, then rode off. It said, 'Go to Zarkali's workshop, now!' I'm so sorry, I panicked and left! I've been hiding in this space all day."

"Someone gave me a key to get here, but now it's jammed," Esa replies. "Let's go to Plan B!"

"Plan B?"

"Yes, come and I'll show you!"

Luckily, Zarkali told Esa about a secret entrance to his workshop through the very same side alley. They step into the alley, and Esa opens an old door to a hidden stairwell that seems to lead nowhere. They climb the staircase slowly, stepping lightly in case it collapses beneath them. Esa shrieks as a spider runs over his foot midway up. The door at the top is locked, but there's an old closet beside it. They quietly creep into the closet, and Esa lifts a loose floorboard to give the boys a direct view into Zarkali's workshop. They slide through the floorboard and fall into the workshop with a thud.

As they drop to the ground, Sol's bottom hits a loose floorboard that flies up in front of him and knocks him on the forehead.

"Ouch!" he screams. "Help me up Sol!" But Esa's eyes are fixed to the ground beneath the floorboard. He kneels over and starts digging through a pile of old leather scrolls covered in cobwebs and insect skeletons, throwing them behind his back.

"What's this?" he cries with excitement.

Sol lifts himself up and helps Esa with the digging. More scrolls, some maps, an old shoe, a gold ring… and the Saphaea.

"Wow!" the boys gasp together, holding it tightly and looking around, as if someone is watching them.

Just then, there's a loud knock at the door. Knock, knock, knock.

The boys peek out the window to see a hasty Zarkali trying to find his keys in his great cloak. They rush to open the door for him, and he comes sweeping in and walks directly to the floorboard, noticing the mess around it. "Do you have the Saphaea?"

"Y-yes Sir!" says Sol with amazement, handing it over to Zarkali. "We thought it was missing!"

"No, my boy. I hid it here and told Aleho that because I was afraid he was the thief! It's been here all along!"

THE END